I Can Read Comics introduces children to the world of graphic novel storytelling and encourages visual literacy in emerging readers. Comics inspire reader engagement unlike any other format. T ask readers to infer and answer questions, like:

1. What do I read first? Image or text?
2. Why is this word balloon shaped this way, and that word balloon shaped that way?
3. Why is a character making that facial expression? Are they happy, angry, excited, sad?

From the comics your child reads with you to the first comic they r their own, there are **I Can Read Comics** for every stage of reading:

LEVEL 1

Simple stories for shared reading.

LEVEL 2

Engaging stories for children reading on their own.

LEVEL 3

Complex stories for independent readers.

The magic of graphic novel storytelling lies between the gutters.
Unlock the magic with…

I Can Read Comics!

Visit **ICanRead.com** for information on enriching your child's reading experience.

I Can Read *Comics* Cartooning Basics

Panel
A moment in time

Gutter
The space between panels

Tier
One row of panels

Word Balloons
When someone talks, thinks, whispers, or screams, their words go in here:

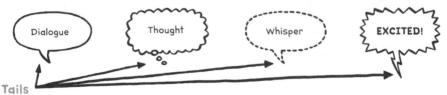

Dialogue

Thought

Whisper

EXCITED!

Tails
Point to whoever is talking / thinking / whispering / screaming / etc.

A quick how-to-read comics guide:

In a **panel**, read the text on the **left** first.

Then, read the text on the right.

Remember to...
Read the text along with the image, paying close attention to the character's acting, the action, and/or the scene. Every little detail matters!

No dialogue? No problem!
If there is no dialogue within a panel, take the time to read the image. Visual cues are just as important as text, so don't forget about them!

On a page, **start here**, in the **top left** corner!

After that, read the panel immediately to the **right**.

When you're done up there, come down here and read **this** panel next!

ME NEXT! ME NEXT!

You're almost there...

YOU MADE IT! You just read a comic page!

YAY!

To Nellie —S.R.

HarperAlley is an imprint of HarperCollins Publishers.
I Can Read® and I Can Read Book® are trademarks of HarperCollins Publishers.

Fish and Sun
Copyright © 2021 by Sergio Ruzzier
All rights reserved. Printed in the United States of America.
No part of this book may be used or reproduced in any manner whatsoever without written permission except in the case of brief quotations embodied in critical articles and reviews. For information address HarperCollins Children's Books, a division of HarperCollins Publishers, 195 Broadway, New York, NY 10007.
www.icanread.com

Library of Congress Control Number: 2021931870
ISBN 978-0-06-307664-8 (trade bdg.) — ISBN 978-0-06-307663-1 (pbk.)

Book design by Rick Farley
21 22 23 24 25 CWM 10 9 8 7 6 5 4 3 2 ❖ First Edition

FISH and SUN

by Sergio Ruzzier

HARPER
alley

An Imprint of HarperCollins Publishers

And it's dark
and cold here.
I'm going out.

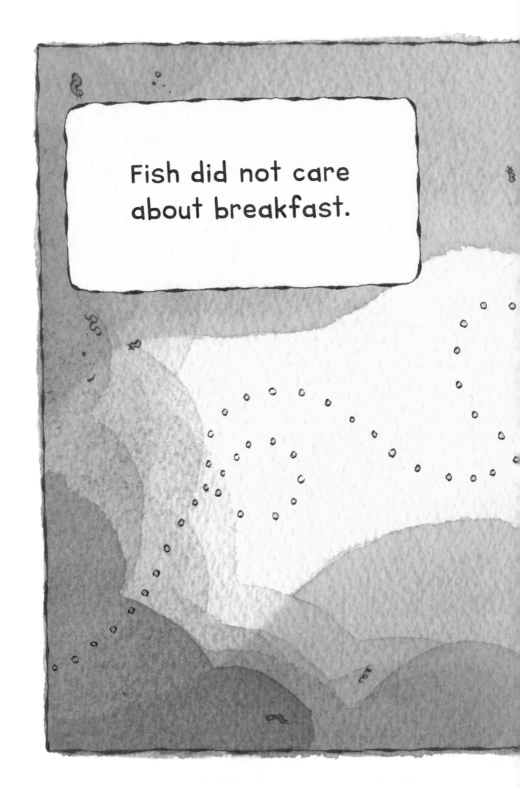

Fish did not care
about breakfast.

Fish cared about light,
being warm,
and not being bored.

But outside
it was also dark
and cold
and boring.

Then, all of a sudden...

23

But Sun was gone.
All was dark
and cold
and boring
again.

That night,
Fish dreamed that
all was dark and cold
and boring.

The day after,
Fish swam all the way out.
But Sun was not there.

Then, all of a sudden...